A Single Mom's Tragedy

NO MORE LULLABIES

On Newsstands Now:

TRUE STORY
and
TRUE CONFESSIONS
Magazines

True Story and *True Confessions* are the world's largest and best-selling women's romance magazines. They offer true-to-life stories to which women can relate.

Since 1919, the iconic *True Story* has been an extraordinary publication. The magazine gets its inspiration from the hearts and minds of women, and touches on those things in life that a woman holds close to her heart, like love, loss, family and friendship.

True Confessions, a cherished classic first published in 1922, looks into women's souls and reveals their deepest secrets.

To subscribe, please visit our website:
www.TrueRenditionsLLC.com or call **(212) 922-9244**

To find the TRUES at your local store, please visit:
www.WheresMyMagazine.com

A Single Mom's Tragedy

NO MORE LULLABIES

From the Editors
Of *True Story* And
True Confessions

Published by True Renditions, LLC

True Renditions, LLC
105 E. 34th Street, Suite 141
New York, NY 10016

ISBN: 978-1-938877-72-8

Visit us on the web at www.truerenditionsllc.com.

Chapter 1

There was a noticeable tremor in my voice and hands as I carefully set the pregnancy test on the sink counter. I turned my back to the test before speaking to my sister, Jessica. "Let's not look until the timer goes off," I said.

"Sounds like a good idea," Jessica said, turning her back as well. But the look she slanted my way was filled with the same fear and anticipation that I was feeling. "Do you want me to cross my fingers?"

I hesitated, before shaking my head. "No. I can't honestly say I'll be disappointed if it's positive."

"Hilary . . . have you thought about this? I mean, Mom and Dad are going to go through the roof."

"It's not their life, it's mine. Besides, I graduate next week. It's not like I'll have to drop out of high school."

Big talk for such a scared little girl. I knew that my parents had high hopes for me. They wanted me to go to college, become a doctor or a lawyer. No, it wasn't their anger I feared; it was their disappointment, and I knew there would be lots and lots of disappointment.

Jessica, being the wonderful sister that she had become since we both had matured, tried to tease me out of my terrorized state.

"I can't believe you might have a baby before I do. I'm three years older—no fair!"

Without missing a beat, I said, "Okay, you can have the baby."

"Yeah, right." She sighed and started to sneak a peak, but I grabbed her shoulder and jerked her back around. "I can't stand the suspense!"

"Which is exactly why you've always sneaked downstairs and opened your presents on Christmas Eve. You couldn't stand to wait, even a few more hours."

My sister shrugged, but I saw her lips twitch. "If God made everyone the same, life would be boring. Isn't that what Mom always says?"

"Yeah, she said that every time you made an A and I made a B, and every time you made the cheerleading squad and I didn't, and every time—"

"Okay, okay!" Jessica protested. "I see you haven't grown out of your very silly jealousy."

"It wasn't jealousy," I denied, which was only a tiny lie. I was jealous of Jessica, but I loved her, too. "It was envy. I have a right to be envious."

I felt her shoulder start to ease sideways and shoved it back. "It shouldn't be long, now. Just wait, and we'll both look at it at the same time. Try not to scream no matter what, okay? Mom and Dad are downstairs." I had to chuckle as Jessica clamped a premature hand over her mouth, then tried to speak through it.

"If it's positive, what do you think Myles will say?"

Miraculously, I understood her muffled question. And it shot cold fear through me. I tried to bluff, but I rarely got anything over on Jessica.

"He told me once that he wanted to have lots of kids."

It was true. I just didn't think he meant the moment he graduated high school. The really scary part was we'd only been dating four months.

Jessica seemed to read my mind. "You haven't known each other very long."

"Just all through high school," I corrected defensively. "Just because we didn't sleep together until recently, doesn't mean I didn't know him before. Myles is a great guy. I thought you liked him."

"I do, I do." She dropped her hand and began to chew her thumbnail. "It's just that I know how guys can change when you drop a bomb like this on them. You think they're sweet and responsible and that they love you; then they turn into this person you don't know."

I gaped at her. "You sound like you know what you're talking about! Is there something you haven't told me?" I was geared to be mad, thinking she might have a secret of that magnitude.

She shook her head vigorously, sending her hair dancing. She was tall and curvy in all the right places.

Night and day, Mom had once said. I knew she hadn't meant to hurt my feelings, but the hurt was there. I wasn't blind; I knew Jessica was a bombshell, while I was a mouse. Sure, I'd filled out and Myles told me at least once a day that I was beautiful, but I knew I was at the very most, passably cute.

"Swear you won't repeat what I'm about to tell you?" Jessica demanded.

I solemnly crossed my heart.

"It's about Laurel. Last year, she got pregnant."

There was no way I could hide my shock. Laurel was the daughter of our pastor, and Jessica's best friend.

"No way!"

"Yes, way. She thought Evan would marry her, but he skipped town and joined the army."

"So she . . ?"

Jessica nodded. "Had an abortion, yes. Her parents never found out."

"You went with her?"

"Yeah. It was awful. She cried all the way there, and all the way

2

back." She shuddered. "After that, I double-checked my birth control pills every day."

"Poor Laurel," I murmured. Suddenly, I squared my shoulders and shot Jessica a steely look. "But if you told me that story hoping to talk me into an abortion, you wasted your breath. If I'm pregnant—"

As if on cue, the timer went off. Instead of turning around, Jessica and I froze, staring at each other. We couldn't seem to move. "I don't want to look," I whispered.

"Me, neither," she whispered back, her expression agonized.

Her hand crept out to capture mine. As one, we slowly turned around. Still in sync, our heads bowed, our gazes dropping to the pregnancy test lying on the counter.

I closed my eyes very tightly, a tremor shooting through my entire body. "Oh, God. Am I imagining things, sis?"

"No." Jessica's voice was a croak. "It's positive. Congratulations, Hilary. You're going to have a baby. . . ." Her voice trailed off to a whisper. She pulled me against her and held me as we both cried.

Finally, I pulled myself together and stepped back. I managed a watery smile.

"I'll be eighteen next month. I already have a summer job lined up at the clinic. If they kick me out, I can make it without them."

"They won't kick you out . . . I don't think." It was clear she wasn't at all as sure as she wanted to be. "Dad's a pharmacist. He has to realize that condoms do break on occasion."

I rolled my eyes, unable to stop the heat that flashed over my face. "I can just hear that conversation now. I've never even discussed my period with Dad."

"Mom will understand. After all, she's said more than once that you were a surprise."

"Yeah, and not a very good one."

Jessica gave me a little shake. "Hey, normally I'd tell you to can the self-pity, but in this case, it just might work. Remind Mom of how happy she wound up being with her little surprise."

I couldn't help rolling my eyes again, even while I fought another flood of tears.

"She probably won't hear me because she'll be too busy telling me how much she sacrificed for me, and how disappointed she is in me."

We talked until dawn. By that time, I had decided to break the news to Myles before I told my parents. I was definitely not looking forward to it.

Chapter 2

Myles stared at me as if I were a stranger. We had started high school together. He'd moved to our town from Columbus, and I had been nominated to show him to his classes and introduce him to the teachers on his first day. I'd had a crush on him then, but he hadn't seemed to notice me. Not that I blamed him—I was not only a late bloomer, but incredibly shy.

When he finally did notice me three years later, I wasn't so naive I didn't realize that he noticed me because he'd gone through every other girl in our school. He swore it wasn't the reason, that he'd been saving the best for last. I had pretended to believe him and pray that I'd get lucky for once in my life, and that Myles really would fall in love with me.

But on the night I told him I was pregnant, Jessica's warning came back to me. Myles changed before my very eyes, becoming distant, suspicious, and finally, angry.

"Did you do it on purpose?"

Something about the snide way he asked the question made me wonder if this was the first time a girl had told him she was going to have his baby.

Determined to remain calm—even if he didn't—I said, "Of course not. You remember when the condom broke, and I believe it was on you at the time. How could that have been my fault?"

"Well it wasn't mine!" he cried, sounding like a petulant little boy.

My hopes began to fall at a rapid rate. I blinked back the sting of tears. "Myles, I'm not trying to trap you into marriage. This is the new millennium, and even if it wasn't, women have been raising kids by themselves for a long time now. I'm just telling you because I thought you had a right to know."

I swallowed a big ball of disappointment, determined not to break down and make him think I wanted his pity. I was hoping he would confess that he loved me and wanted to be a part of my baby's life, but I was also prepared for the opposite.

Or at least I thought I was.

In a hateful, totally alien voice, Myles said, "I wished you hadn't told me!"

Shaking inside and feeling sick, I gathered my purse and jacket and started to get out of the car. We were parked at a fast-food restaurant, but I think I would have walked to the moon just to get away from the awful stranger Myles had become. If he didn't want to acknowledge his own child, then I didn't want to hear anymore of his hurtful comments.

He stopped me just as I closed the car door. "Wait! Hilary . . . come back to the car. I'm sorry."

I hesitated long enough to regain some of my dignity before I got back inside. With my chin held high, I stared out the windshield and waited. If he wanted to talk, he could talk. I wasn't going to push him into anything. Despite whatever Myles might have thought, I had made plans to have my baby without him.

A long, tense silence passed before he said, "I need some time to think."

I had to bite my tongue to keep from making a snide comment about his worn-out cliché. Time to think? Well, as far as I was concerned, he could take the rest of his life! My anger and hurt grew by the second. Between clenched teeth, I said, "Take as long as you'd like. You can also take me home, unless you'd like me to walk."

"Have you told your parents?"

The most I could muster was a brief shake of my head.

"Will they kick you out?"

What did he care? I shrugged, still not looking at him. I felt cold inside, and very lonely. Thank God Jessica was on spring break from college. I don't know if I could have been so brave without her by my side.

"What will you do if they kick you out?"

I looked at him then, froze him with a cold look. Only when I saw the shame in his eyes, did I look back at the windshield? My voice matched my eyes. "I'll take care of myself and my baby."

Myles put his hand on the keys, but he didn't start the car. Hesitantly, he asked, "Have you thought about an abortion?"

The word sounded ugly and loud in the confines of the car. It felt that way deep inside me, too. Without the slightest doubt, I said, "No."

"Will you—"

"No. Take me home, please."

"Hilary—"

"Just take me home," I said between gritted teeth. "Unless you want me to puke all over your car."

He started the car and burned rubber getting out of the parking lot.

"Hilary! How could you be so careless with your life?"

My gaze met Jessica's. It wasn't exactly what we thought Mom would say, but it was close enough. "I didn't get pregnant on purpose . . . just like you didn't get pregnant with me on purpose."

Mom's blue eyes narrowed to warning slits. "It isn't the same, and you know it! I was married to your dad, and we already had one child. You haven't even graduated high school."

"I graduate next week, and I already have a job lined up. I still plan on going to college."

With a snort, Mom turned her back on me. I saw her wipe at her eyes, and the guilt clenched my stomach like an iron fist. The anger I could handle; it was the hurt that I dreaded.

"Wesley, you talk to her," she said to my dad.

Wesley and Evette Laughlin weren't the worst parents in the world to have, but they weren't the warmest, either. My mother raised us without missing a beat in her climb up the corporate ladder with the company she worked for, and my dad was a well-respected pharmacist with his own business. Although we were considered middle class, I don't think my mother ever felt satisfied with our stature. She wanted more, and she wanted more for her daughters, too.

My dad was braced in the doorway. He rubbed his eyes and heaved a great sigh. "Hilary, what your mother is trying to say is that if you want to have an abortion or give the baby up, we'll stand behind you one hundred percent."

Very softly, I said, "And if I want to keep it?"

Silence. I avoided looking at Jessica, afraid I'd lose it and break down. Showing weakness at this point would have been devastating.

When it didn't look as if either of them would speak, I stood, deciding it was time to tell them exactly what I planned to do, whether they approved or not.

"I'm keeping the baby. I don't know yet where Myles stands in this, but I'm going to keep the baby. If you want me to, I'll get my own place as soon as I can afford it."

Mom turned around, her eyes red-rimmed and sad. "I think that would be best, Hilary. I don't think I could stand to watch you throw your future away."

Jessica could stay quiet no longer. She came to stand beside me, deliberately putting her arm around my shoulders. "Mom, Dad, I don't think you've had time to think about what you're saying. In this day and age, women have babies all the time. They manage to work—just as you did, Mom—and go to school. It's not the end of the world we're talking about; we're talking about a new life."

Mom burst into tears and raced from the room. Dad sighed again and mumbled something about starting supper.

Jessica squeezed my shoulders and gave me an encouraging smile. "See, that wasn't so bad, was it? Don't worry, they'll come around."

Chapter 3

They didn't come around. Although they attended my graduation, they didn't smile or congratulate me. Later, at home, they presented me with a check, a graduation present. I didn't have to look at their set, cold faces to know what they meant for me to do with that check.

The next day, Jessica and I went apartment hunting. We lucked out and found one three blocks from the clinic where I would began my summer job as receptionist. It was small, but it was mine, and I could afford it.

Jessica helped me decorate the apartment and move in. Since we'd both gotten used cars for our sixteenth birthdays, I didn't have to worry about transportation.

Myles had been ominously distant since I told him the news. He spoke to me at graduation, but we were no longer dating. I wondered if he was still taking "time," or if this was my answer. Most of the time, I succeeded in putting him from my mind. I had plenty to keep me busy, with pregnancy, my new job, and my new apartment.

My job started the following Monday after I moved into my new apartment. Jessica, who was still angry with our parents, stayed with me over the weekend. I was constantly amazed at how close we'd become now that we weren't fighting over clothes or our parents' attention or a hundred and one things sisters fight over.

Working at the clinic turned out to be the highlight of my summer and my pregnancy. Dr. Bernard was a general practitioner, and although he didn't specialize in obstetrics, he agreed to be my physician as long as no complications arose. The nurses and other staff treated me like a fragile doll, constantly giving me advice and prompting me to put up my feet even before I was showing.

The downside to working for Dr. Bernard was the fact that he was also my parents' doctor.

One day, after I'd worked at the clinic for a couple of months, he called me into his office. I could tell by the grim set of his mouth that he didn't have good news.

Alarm shot through me. I clutched my gently mounded stomach. "Is something wrong with the baby?" My voice came out all squeaky and scared.

Dr. Bernard's eyes widened. He came up out of his chair and rushed over to me, leading me to the chair in front of his desk. "No, no!" When I was settled and my heart rate had begun to return to normal, he resumed his seat.

He steepled his hands before speaking. Obviously, he was searching for words. "Um, I had a talk with Wesley and Evette last night at a barbecue fund-raiser."

"Oh." My heart rate settled into an uneasy rhythm. "I guess they talked your ears off about their terrible daughter."

He shook his head, smiling benignly. "No, no, they didn't talk bad about you at all, Hilary. They're just concerned for your future." He cleared his throat and suddenly found his fingers interesting. "They, um, wanted me to talk to you."

I clenched my hands together in my lap, striving to keep the sharpness from my voice. Dr. Bernard was a sweet man; he couldn't be blamed for my parents' meddling. "What about?" As if I didn't know. But I pretended I didn't, out of respect for Dr. Bernard.

"Well, they wanted me to make certain you understand that it isn't too late to abort the baby." He fiddled with the pencil holder, his cheeks reddening. "I, um, promised them I would help out in any way I could."

My respect for Dr. Bernard sank several notches. "Meaning you would perform the abortion?" I asked, surprised to hear my own voice sounding even and without emotion.

Dr. Bernard shot a nervous glance at the door before he said, "Um, yes, I would, if that's what you wanted."

I took several deep breaths, stunned at the realization that my parents had coaxed Dr. Bernard into agreeing to do something illegal.

"Of course, it would be called a D&C on record," he added lamely.

Coldly, I pointed out, "Everyone knows I'm going to have a baby, so I don't think that would fly."

"My staff signed a confidentiality contract."

"I'm having this baby, Dr. Bernard. I thought you were happy for me." Stiffly, I stood. Inside, my gut was churning with hurt and dread. I needed my job, but I could always find another one. "I'll clean out my desk."

Dr. Bernard looked alarmed. "No, no! Don't quit on me! I was just trying to help out." He shook his head, his eyes filled with regret and a bit of shame.

"I'm sorry, Hilary. I realize now that you really want to have this baby. I guess I thought—" He shook his head again. "I guess it doesn't matter what I thought. You're eighteen, old enough to know what you want. Can—can we just forget this conversation ever took place?"

Although I was still seething inside, I nodded. Dr. Bernard had apologized and seemed sincere, and not only did I love my job, but I needed it. As long as he didn't pressure me, I would do my best to forget the conversation took place.

I was halfway down the hall when I remembered I needed to be off the following Monday. It was my birthday, and Jessica was taking me shopping for maternity clothes. She insisted, despite my protests that I could buy my own. Secretly, I was grateful. It was hard to stretch my income to include anything extra.

My mind was on other things, so I didn't think to knock as I opened the office door to poke my head inside. I caught Dr. Bernard in the act of popping a pill from a prescription bottle he held in his hand. I might not have thought much of it if he hadn't looked so guilty.

"Um, I'm sorry. I was just going to let you know that I wouldn't be in on Monday. It's my birthday." I was flustered, uncertain if I should pretend I hadn't seen him, or ask if he was seriously ill.

I opted for discretion. Despite his guilty look, Dr. Bernard didn't seem like the pill-popping type. But then, I was only eighteen. What did I know? One thing I did know, it wasn't any of my business.

"Fine, fine." His grin looked pained. He indicated the bottle in his hand, and I noticed that it was trembling. "High blood pressure. My wife calls every day to remind me to take my medicine."

"Oh." Well, that explained it . . . except I didn't believe him. It wasn't anything he did or said; it was just instinctive. Dr. Bernard had just lied to me. I would have bet my next paycheck.

I tried to put the incident from my mind, but it continued to bug me. Was I that naive about people? Obviously I had been wrong about Myles being a responsible, caring man. I hadn't had so much as a phone call from him in three months.

Chapter 4

When Monday rolled around, Jessica had a special surprise for me. At least, I believe she meant well. She brought Mom along on our shopping trip.

After not speaking for two months, I wasn't inclined to make the first move, so I was cool for the first hour. Jessica found herself on the sharp end of a few dirty looks from me before she finally stopped dead on the sidewalk and threw up her hands.

"I've had enough! Both of you; kiss and make up right now! You are mother and daughter, for Pete's sake."

I stared at the sidewalk. Mom stared at her shoes.

Jessica grabbed both our arms and yanked us together. Clumsily, we hugged mostly to appease her, I suspected, and I might have left it at that if I hadn't caught the sheen of tears in Mom's eyes.

To my chagrin, I burst into tears. Before I knew it we were hugging and kissing and crying all over one another. But Mom being Mom, wouldn't leave well enough alone.

She pulled back and gripped my shoulders, nearly nose to nose to me. I don't think I remember ever seeing her so fierce.

"Honey, are you absolutely certain you want to have this baby?"

After the reunion we'd just had, her words were like a slap in the face. I actually jerked my head back. "If you hate kids so much, why did you have us?"

Her face crumpled. It was a moment before she could speak again. "I love you and your sister more than life itself, but I just want you to know that it's possible to be happy without having children. A lot of women are choosing careers over kids these days."

"I'm not one of those women," I said coldly. "Either we drop the subject, or we part ways right here. Mother. I love you, but I can't handle fighting with you every time we're together."

She surprised me by relenting, looking almost resigned and a little scared, which totally puzzled me. Why would my mother be afraid for me to have a child? Was there something she wasn't telling me? Something I needed to know? And if there was, why wasn't she telling me?

I swallowed hard, telling myself that I had to ask the question even if I didn't really want to know the answer. "Mom—"

"I'm sorry, Hilary," she said in a rush, almost as if she knew what I was going to ask and wanted to stop me. "Consider the subject closed." When she smiled, I knew without a doubt that it wasn't sincere. "When is your first ultrasound? I'd like to be there."

It took me a while to relax after that. The fact that Mom made a three-hundred-and-sixty degree turn about the baby left me tense and completely confused—and suspicious. How could I trust her after the hell she'd put me through? Was she really okay with the baby now? I even considered that my mother was suffering from some type of mental break down or something.

I kept silent through lunch as she regaled us about our childhood adventures, some of which I wasn't even aware she knew. Like the time Jessica convinced me to swallow a half-dozen pennies, and the time Jessica broke Mom's cookie jar and blamed it on me. Mom confessed that she knew who had been the real culprit, although she had sent us both to our rooms.

I was in the dressing room of a department store trying on a maternity outfit when Mom dropped the bomb.

"Hilary, you can move back in if you'd like."

At first, I thought I'd heard her wrong. I wiggled my fingers in my ears and pulled aside the curtain. "What did you say, Mom?"

This time, her smile looked genuine. "I said you can move back in with us, if you'd like."

When I shot Jessica a dumbfounded look, she gave her shoulders a bewildered shake, letting me know this was the first she'd heard of it, too.

Finally, I found my tongue. "Um, that's generous, Mom, but I think I like living on my own." I smiled to take the sting out of my rejection. "Makes me feel like a grown-up."

Mom's smile faded a little, but that didn't stop her from dropping a second bomb. "Will you at least take a year off before you start college? I'm worried that you'll get too stressed with school, work, and taking care of the baby."

I turned around to face the full-length mirror in the dressing room to hide my total confusion. I even felt of my forehead to see of I was running a fever and might be hallucinating. Was it really that simple? Had Mom seen that I was determined to have the baby and completely come around?

Or was I losing my ever-loving mind?

Jessica appeared at my shoulder, whispering in my ear, and making me jump. "Do you remember the time I told you that I didn't believe in aliens?"

I met her glance in the mirror and nodded.

She leaned closer. "Well, I've changed my mind. I think an alien took our real mother up into a space ship and replaced her with one of them."

"Ha, ha," I said, but shakily. Not in a million years would I tell

11

her that I almost believed her explanation. Something had definitely changed. Instantly and drastically.

"Hilary? Are you listening to me? What are you two girls whispering about, anyway?"

We jumped apart as if she'd screamed at us. I suspect both of us looked equally guilty. Jessica hurried out of the dressing room, leaving me to face the music alone.

"Yes, Mom, I heard you. In fact, I had already decided to wait until next year to start college." My chin came up in a gesture of defense. Old habits died hard. "I want to be home with my baby for at least six months before I turn him over to a stranger."

"Him?"

Was that a tremor in her voice? I frowned and shook my head, deciding my hormones were definitely making me paranoid. "Just an expression, Mom. Him or her, I meant. I'll take either one."

"Well, I hope you have a girl."

Three hours earlier, she hadn't wanted me to have a baby. Now, she wanted a girl. Dizziness washed over me. I reached out to brace my hand against the wall, creating instant panic around me.

"What's wrong, darling?"

"Hilary?" Jessica's sharp voice forced me to focus. "Are you going to faint?"

"Um, no, I just got a little dizzy." I looked pointedly at Mom, then back to Jessica. My sister got the message, all right. She looked as confused as I felt, which made me feel better. I wasn't going insane unless Jessica happened to be going insane with me, and what were the odds?

The rest of the afternoon proved to be just as bizarre. Mom bought dozens of girl things for the baby. Pink bed sets, curtains, and cute little frilly dresses. When I asked her if she was being a little presumptuous, she laughed and told me it was more like wishful thinking.

"You can always exchange it if you have a boy," she said.

Yeah, but wouldn't it be easier just to wait until after my ultrasound, when we would hopefully find out for certain the sex of my baby? I didn't voice the question, unwilling to put a damper on Mom's bubbling, scary mood.

Chapter 5

Lady luck seemed to be smiling on me over the course of the next few months. Mom and Dad were finally—and still eerily—acting like expectant grandparents, Dr. Bernard offered me a full-time job at the clinic, at least until I started back to college, and Myles came to see me.

The fact that he came to visit me the day before my first ultrasound instantly aroused my suspicion. I knew that my sister, or my parents, for that matter, was perfectly capable of calling him and laying on the guilt.

Still, my heart gave a hopeful leap when I opened my apartment door to find him standing in the hall. I braced myself at the sight of his sheepish grin and willed my fluttering heart to be still.

"Myles," I said, as if I didn't want to throw my arms around him.

"Hilary . . . you look great." His gaze lingered on my little basketball tummy.

I saw his eyes go soft, and the flicker of hope inside of me leaped higher. "Um, do you want to come in?" He was the father of my baby, so the least I could do was hear him out.

The moment the door shut behind him, he blurted out, "I've been a bastard to you, and I'm sorry."

Outwardly cool, I pointed to my stomach. "Don't apologize to me, apologize to him."

Myles's eyes went wide. "Him? It's a boy?"

I blew out a frustrated sigh. "No, I need to stop doing that." Then I realized that he couldn't have known about the ultrasound if he thought I already knew the sex of our baby. "I find out tomorrow, hopefully. I'm having an ultrasound."

He shoved his hands in his pockets, apparently mesmerized by my protruding stomach. "Could I come with you?"

Be still my beating heart. I managed to shrug as if it didn't matter. "The room will be a little crowded. Mom and Jessica want to be there, too."

"I don't mind."

"Why the sudden change of heart?" Me and my curiosity. I just had to get to the truth before my hopes went through the ceiling. Did I love Myles? I thought I did. I also believed the least we could do for our child is to find out if we did.

"I've been doing some thinking," Myles said. "You sort of caught me off guard, you know."

"Yeah, the positive pregnancy test sort of caught me off guard, too." Which was the truth, although I hadn't reacted as badly as Myles had. "So what happens now?" I was letting him know in my own subtle way that I wasn't into playing games. Either he was in, or he was out. If he was out, I preferred he stay that way.

"You think maybe we could start dating again, for starters?" he suggested tentatively.

I pretended to consider his question before I said yes.

"And I'd really like to be there when you get your ultrasound thingy."

My smile came naturally. I felt suddenly giddy and more than a little ashamed of myself for giving in so easily. "Jessica probably won't be nice," I warned.

Myles grinned, reminding me that he could charm the pants—literally—from a woman. "I can handle Jessica."

And I believed him, because he certainly handled me. I think that's when I knew that I did love Myles.

The day of my ultrasound was a day to remember, for more than one reason. I found out I was going to have a boy, and Mom and Dad presented me with a house. Yes, a house. They were rather embarrassed when they told me it needed work and that it wasn't fancy. They had inherited it from my Dad's great aunt several years earlier, they told me, and had been debating on what to do with it.

The moment I set eyes on the small two-bedroom frame house, I fell in love. I saw beyond the peeling exterior, the broken screen door, the warped porch, and the overgrown yard. It was a home for me and my baby, and possibly Myles.

I've heard people say they feared happiness, but I was too young and too naive to be afraid. Myles proposed, and we got married two days before I went into labor. I gave birth to a seven pound, two ounce beautiful baby boy we named Jacob Ashton, and we brought him home to an adorable little house my entire family had pitched in to help remodel.

My life was almost perfect. I'd even gotten over my surprise at Mom's change of heart. When I saw her with Jacob, I found it hard to remember a time when Mom practically begged me to have an abortion.

She took a long vacation from her job and came over nearly every day, insisting on helping me with housework and taking care of Jacob for a couple of hours so that I could nap or read. Dad was just as goofy over his grandson, and my heart nearly swelled to bursting each time I saw them together.

Chapter 6

The darkest hour of my life happened the night Myles and I sneaked away for a short honeymoon when Jacob turned six weeks old. Mom and Dad stayed with Jacob at our house.

They say the blast was tremendous, caused by a gas leak beneath the house that had been building for days. I remember each and every word the fire chef told me as if it happened yesterday. The words sometimes replay inside my head like a song you just can't get out.

Only it was a nightmare of a song, a haunting, terrible litany of words that nearly drove me insane with grief and shock.

"There's been an explosion at your house, Mrs. MacKenzie," the disembodied voice on the phone had told me. "Your mother's okay, but your father is hurt pretty badly. They're taking him to the hospital." I had heard my mother crying hysterically in the background, but the sound hardly registered.

When the call came, Myles and I had just finished making love. We were lying in a king-sized hotel bed in a ritzy hotel downtown. I had a champagne headache, and Myles was dozing beside me.

I don't think I've ever known such terror, or ever will again. I reached out to shake Myles awake as I asked the fearful question, "Jacob? Is my baby okay?"

The silence made me stop breathing. I gripped the phone so hard I heard the plastic crack.

"Ma'am? You and your husband need to come to the hospital. Your mother says she'll meet you there."

But I didn't care about my mother, or my father, for that matter. I wanted to know about my baby. The man wouldn't answer me, and I hated him for that. I wanted to reach through the phone and curl my fingers around his neck and squeeze the answer out of him.

Beside me, Myles stirred awake. He sat up, trying to ease out of the death grip I had on his shoulder. "Honey? What is it?"

Faintly, I said, "Our house blew up." To the voice on the phone, I ordered coldly, "Put my mother on the phone." No please to it. I was beyond manners. I needed information, and I realized the man wasn't going to give it to me.

My mother was sobbing so hard, I was afraid she wouldn't be able to answer me. "Mother, shut up!" I shouted, uncaring how disrespectful I was being. She was obviously hysterical, and I needed her to tell me that my baby was safe. "How is Jacob?"

"Oh, God," she sobbed hoarsely. "They—they said—oh, God!"

I handed the phone to Myles and slid from the bed. "Make her tell you what happened to our baby," I ordered. I began to get dressed, holding myself together by a thread. Jacob was okay, I told myself over and over again, but not really believing it. Mom hadn't said the words—couldn't say them—and deep down inside, I knew the reason.

Through a fog of shock, I heard Myles calmly ask Mom about Jacob. I refused to look at his face. Perversely, now that I was faced with finding out the truth, I delayed accepting it.

In the next few moments, I would find out if my baby was all right or how badly injured he was after the explosion.

"There's been an explosion at your house, Mrs. MacKenzie," a disembodied voice said. "Your mother's okay, but your father is hurt pretty badly. They're taking him to the hospital." Evette's hysterical crying could be heard in the background.

"Jacob? Is my baby okay?" Hilary asked.

Hilary spoke to her mother on the phone briefly. Then Myles and Hilary rushed to the hospital to find out about their son. . . .

The emergency room vibrated with a certain morbid energy, but I had eyes only for my mother—and the answers she could give me. I found her sitting by herself in an uncomfortable-looking plastic chair. She was bent forward, hugging herself. Her face was blotched red, and her normally styled hair was wind blown and frizzy.

The shock of seeing her so unraveled evoked a moan of terror and dread, but the moan got locked in my throat. Myles was behind me, then beside me, taking my cold hand as we approached my distraught mother. People stared at us, but I ignored them. They were there for scrapes, broken bones, and the flu. I was there to find out if my baby boy was alive or dead.

She looked up at us, blinking as if in a daze. I don't think she recognized us right away. Her makeup-streaked eyes filled with tears. She stumbled to her feet. Myles shot out an arm to catch her and hold her steady. She took two tottering steps toward me and fell into my arms.

It was instinctive to catch her, otherwise, she might have fallen to the floor. My entire body felt numb, unreal. Dead. I was useless in the way of comfort—seeking only terrible knowledge.

For a moment, I let her cry on my shoulder, feeling the warmth of her tears as they soaked the silk blouse I'd bought just for my honeymoon. Then her time was up.

I grabbed her shoulders and yanked her back, staring fiercely into her face. My voice was like a long, cold steel whip.

"Where is Jacob?" I shook her without giving her time to answer. "Where is he, Mother? I left him in your care!"

Her face started to crumple, so I shook her again. My normally in-charge mother, so cool and controlling, couldn't seem to answer a question. I could summon no sympathy. I didn't care if she was on the verge of an aneurysm. I wanted an answer! Her trembling lips moved. A whisper of sound emerged. I leaned close to catch her words.

"The—the blast—they haven't found a body. Jacob's body." She sobbed once, then gathered a huge breath, her reddened eyes swimming in tears. "Your father—"

I slapped her. Hard. The crack of my hand reverberated through the room, and a dead silence followed. We had everyone's attention then, from sniffling toddlers to the old and deaf, but I didn't care.

With eerie calm, I spoke. "I don't care about Dad right now. Tell me what happened to Jacob."

Mom shot Myles a beseeching look, as if searching for an ally. I grabbed her chin and forced her to look at me again. I'm certain my crushing fingers left bruises on my mother's face, but I wasn't myself.

She finally spilled the story, in a halting, half-sobbing whine of a voice that grated on my nerves like glass on steel.

"I ran to the store to get Wesley some ice cream. The chocolate one with nuts. You know that's his favorite."

My fingers tightened in warning. She swallowed hard and continued.

"I was just getting out of the car when I heard this awful sound, an explosion. I was thrown against the car; I think it might have knocked me out for a moment or two. When next I opened my eyes, the house was blazing. I saw your father stumbling out of the door. That's where he collapsed. I had to drag him to safety."

At that moment, I think I came really close to having the nerve and the strength to strangle her. I hated her so much I could taste the bitterness of it in my mouth.

"You didn't try to get Jacob out?" I wasn't rational. All I could think about was my mother dragging my dad to safety while my helpless baby could have been saved.

Mom cringed from the thick accusation in my voice. "I couldn't, Hilary! The house was on fire! Things were exploding and flying around. I wouldn't have made it back out."

I dropped my hands from her shoulders before I did something I might regret. Later, I realized there was nothing my mother could have done for Jacob, but at the time I wasn't thinking straight.

"Get the car," I said to Myles. "We're going to look for Jacob. Mother said they hadn't found a body, which means the blast could have thrown him from the house. He might still be alive."

Myles started to take my elbow, but dropped his hand quickly when he saw my crazed expression. "I'll meet you out front."

The drive to our house seemed to take a million years. I sat rigidly, one hand gripping the door handle and the other gripping the seat. I wanted to shout and curse at Myles to go faster, but I knew that he was going as fast as he dared. Getting killed wouldn't help Jacob, if he were alive.

Emergency vehicles and fire trucks prevented us from getting close to the house. We left the car in the street and Myles took my hand. We ran past shouting fireman and gawking bystanders. The heat from the blaze scorched my face, but I kept going even when Myles started to pull back.

"Are you crazy?" a fireman shouted at us, waving us frantically back. "Get out of here!"

I ignored him, literally pulling Myles forward. I think I might have walked right into the hellish inferno, taking my husband with me, if two firemen hadn't forcibly blocked our paths.

"My baby's in there!" I shouted as if he were stupid. "We've got to help him!"

Despite his sweat-streaked, blackened face, I saw the sudden pity that bloomed in the fireman's eyes. My fingers curled. I wanted to scratch his eyes out because I knew what he was going to say. I didn't want to hear the words; I wanted to stop him.

"Ma'am, I'm sorry. Nobody left inside could have lived through that." He waved an indicating hand at the fully engulfed house. "If the blast didn't kill him, the smoke did."

Myles took my shoulders and led me away from the heat, but we didn't go far. We sat down by the road and held each other, watching the blaze. I didn't cry. I just sat there, waiting.

Through the long night, we waited. Neighbors brought us coffee and offered us bagels and sandwiches. We took the coffee and shook our heads at the food. I would have gagged if I'd tried to eat anything. It was hard enough getting the coffee down my raw throat. Someone wrapped a warm blanket around us, and another person tucked a thermos of coffee against my leg.

As the sun rose, the fireman managed to put out the last of the flames. There was nothing left, nothing intact except for the bathtub and the sink, and the blackened, warped hulk of the washer and dryer in the laundry room.

I stared, my eyes burned raw from the smoke and the heat, at the room that had been Jacobs. It was completely flattened, nothing but smoking, chard remains of his furniture, his toys, and his bed.

His little body would be nothing but ashes.

The fire chef, looking as if someone had painted his face and neck with black shoe polish, came to kneel before us. Just as before, I was filled with an unjustified rage at the pity in his eyes.

"We didn't find any remains. I'm sorry."

18

My voice was a hoarse croak as I said woodenly: "What about bones? Wouldn't there be bones?"

He shook his head. "Maybe on someone bigger, but on an infant. . . ."

I licked my dry, cracked lips, trying to absorb the terrible information. "But . . . how will we bury our little boy if we don't have a body?"

Myles hugged me tight, his voice shaky with tears. "Don't, honey. Don't torture yourself. It's killing me."

I looked at him, incredulously. "Killing you? Killing you? Our son is dead. Blown to bits. Burned to a crisp."

Even saying the words out loud couldn't penetrate the numbness of my mind and body at that time. I just literally couldn't accept it.

I'd fought my parents to keep Jacob. I had suffered hurt and betrayal from Myles. I had put off college to spend time with my baby.

Now he was gone. Gone. Up in a puff of smoke.

I heard someone giggle, and I remember thinking the sound was off, as if that person had gone a little crazy.

Then I realized that it was me that was giggling. My giggles turned to harsh, braying laughter, and finally, to heartrending sobs that tore at my insides as if someone had reached in with clawed fingers and grabbed my heart.

There is no other pain greater than losing a child. I'll stand before God and everyone and swear to it. Time eventually dulls the pain, but it never goes completely away, and not getting to see my little boy's body lowered into the earth kept me from closure for a long, long time.

I had dreams of finding him in a ditch, or at the base of a tree, snug in his little sleeper. In my dreams, he'd been thrown by the blast and was still alive. I'd cry happy tears, and as I cried over him and hugged him to my breast, he would turn to ashes and blow away in the wind.

From those dreams, I would wake up shaking and crying. The pain was back in full force, the grief nearly killing me. My arms empty and aching.

It was months before I forced myself to realize that Mother couldn't have saved Jacob. But it was even longer before I truly forgave her for not dying with Jacob. Instead he'd died alone.

Dad recovered, but he'd lost most of his hearing in both ears, and his head injury played havoc with his short-term memory. He sold the business and retired early, content to have Mom take care of him.

People tried to console me with the fact that Jacob surely died instantly, that he didn't suffer, but these facts didn't console me. They reminded me of the baby that I'd lost.

Chapter 7

Two years after Jacob's death, I was at his grave replacing the wilted flowers I'd left the week before when Myles came to stand beside me. I went every week, always bringing fresh flowers. At first, Myles went with me, then he began to make excuses. I started to hate him, believing he'd forgotten our son or wanted to forget.

It was spring. A soft, warm breeze blew through the cemetery, carrying the fresh scent of rain. I lifted my face to the sun and closed my eyes, remembering Jacob as I always remembered him.

Myles waited respectfully until I completed my ritual.

"I'm leaving, Hilary. I know this probably isn't a shock to you, but I wanted to let you know. I'll be staying with my parents until I find an apartment."

Before you hate Myles for deserting me, you have to understand that I wasn't the same woman he fell in love with. I was an empty shell, a cold person who couldn't stand to be touched by him or anyone else. I lived. I ate. I went to work and slept, but I wasn't really there—not the way a man needs a woman to be. He'd been patient, more than most, and now he was leaving.

He was right about my not being shocked. I knew he would leave. I had, in fact anticipated, it. I simply didn't blame him. I couldn't look at Myles without thinking about Jacob, without feeling that heart-wrenching pain of grief, so I think we both knew that it was best that he'd leave.

After Myles left, Jessica and Mom bullied me into seeing a therapist. They believed it was high time I got on with my life. Grieving wouldn't bring back my baby, they said, and it had already lost me my husband. I could have explained to them that it wasn't grief that had driven away Myles, but me, but I didn't have the energy.

My therapist and I hit off right away. She told me point blank that she couldn't help me, that only time could do that, but that she could listen. I admired her for that brutal honesty, and as a result, probably got more out of the sessions than I might have otherwise gotten. Another thing I liked about her was the fact that she didn't mention Jacob's name.

It was six months before he came into the conversation, and I brought it up. I think that I felt reluctant to talk about him because this woman was a stranger. She'd never seen my Jacob. Never smelled his baby-powdered skin. Never caressed his baby soft cheeks, or held him when he cried. How could she possibly understand how it felt to lose a child? I found out the day I brought Jacob into our sessions, that she did indeed know how it felt.

"I started college today," I told her. We had discussed my going to college. In the end, I realized it was a good, positive move in the right direction.

"That's great. Meet any hunks?"

I smiled at her teasing remark. I really liked her style. I had decided to enter a physician's assistant program. From our talks, I knew that she wasn't married. I suspected it was because she didn't particularly care for men, but I was never certain. I didn't have the nerve to come right out and ask her.

That day, I felt braver than normal. "Are you asking for me, or for you?"

She laughed, skillfully evading my question and leaving me in the dark. "I take it your parents are ecstatic?"

"Of course. It's what they've always wanted." I tried my best to keep the bitterness out of my voice, but Phylicia was good at her job for a reason; she was sharp.

"Yes, I know, but what's important is what you want, Hilary."

I stared down at my hands, at the blunt, polished nails and the ringless finger. "They didn't want me to keep Jacob," I whispered, speaking his name in her office for the first time. To give her credit, if she was shocked she didn't show it.

"So you blame them for his death?"

"No . . . Yes. I mean, I know it wasn't their fault, and to be honest, they ended up loving him almost as much as I did." I looked at her, blinking at the tears forming. "I know this is probably going to sound stupid, but I can't help thinking that maybe Mom prayed so hard that I wouldn't have the baby that God heard her."

Blunt to the core, Phylicia chided, "Hilary . . . you don't really believe that, do you? Weren't your parents upset when Jacob died?"

"Very," I admitted. "And most of the time, I don't think that way now, but sometimes . . . sometimes, I do."

"Does it make you feel bad?"

"Of course. That's why I try not to think about it." I bowed my head again, swallowing my tears. "The fire left me nothing. Not even a charred rattle by which to remember him."

I heard a thumping noise and looked up to find Phylicia with her fist to her heart, her eyes shimmering with tears. I started to apologize for making her cry, but the sudden raw flash of pain in her eyes stopped me.

That pain wasn't just about Jacob, I realized.

"You remember him in here," she stated, huskily. "You never forget."

My heart thumped against my chest. I recognized that look. It was the look I saw in the mirror every morning. "You've lost someone close to you?"

She nodded. "I would have told you sooner, but I was afraid you'd start charging me, instead of the other way around." Her smile was wobbly. "Maybe it isn't very professional of me, but I've come to think of you as a friend—as well as a patient."

"I feel the same way." I hesitated to pry, but my curiosity was at an all-time high. "Will you tell me what happened? I mean, if it isn't too painful."

She smiled, but it was a sad smile. "I think you know that it's always too painful. Yet, sometimes we need to talk about it, or the knot in our chest just gets bigger and bigger until we feel like it's cutting off our air supply."

I knew exactly how she felt, so I nodded.

"He was five and had just started kindergarten. I let him ride the bus because the other kids in the neighborhood—his playmates—were."

She shook her head as if to rid herself of an ugly memory. "I guess I should have trusted my instincts. Eddie was one of those rambunctious boys who didn't pay attention to where he was going half the time. He dropped his backpack in front of the school bus, spilling his lunch onto the road. I was watching from the window, but I couldn't get the front door open fast enough. The bus driver didn't see him, of course."

She stared off into space, her eyes shiny. "It was one of those freak accidents that you find hard to believe even when someone else is telling it."

Tears flowed freely down my face. I felt her pain as if it were my own. "Didn't the bus have one of those front guards on it?"

"This one didn't. I found out later that the regular bus was in for repairs, and this was an older model. That's what I mean by freak accident, and it's taken me nearly ten years to come to the realization that it was just Eddie's time to go."

She took a deep breath, wiping at her eyes. "You can imagine how much I hated that bus driver. When I heard that he'd taken his own life, I remember that I actually felt better. Isn't that awful?"

"No. You weren't yourself. Grief is like an ugly alien that takes over your mind and your body." I said it with conviction, and I think that was the moment I decided to stop hating everyone for Jacob's death and to start living again, or at least try.

Chapter 8

The following year, I was in a coffee shop studying for midterm when a clumsy man tripped and dumped a steaming cappuccino all over my expensive textbook.

I jumped up, but not before part of the hot liquid dribbled into my lap. Holding my dress away from my body, I glared at the man. "Do you know how much that book cost me?" I demanded.

He grinned, and just like that, my anger drained away. I found my lips twitching, but was determined to hold the smile at bay.

"Sixy-four dollars and ninety-five cents?" he guessed. When my gaze went wide with disbelief, he laughed, and held up his own identical physiology book. While I stood there with my mouth open in shock, he took a bunch of napkins, and wiped up the mess. He promptly switched books, taking the ruined one and tucking it under his armpit.

"There. All better? Can I interest you in a latte?"

My brow shot up. "Only if I get to carry it to the table."

We talked for two hours, had dinner that night, and breakfast the next morning. For the first time in a long time, I didn't think about Jacob.

His name was Stephen Magadan, and he was a year younger than me. He had dark hair and dark brown eyes, and the whitest teeth I've ever seen on a guy.

"Is your father a dentist?" I blurted out, unable to take my eyes from that impressive set of chompers. He laughed, but beneath his tan, I saw a blush coming on.

"Not only pretty, but psychic."

I can't say it was love at first sight, but we spent a lot of time together. Eventually, it was inevitable that we move in together. I told Stephen about my first marriage and about Jacob.

He cried. That was the moment I fell in love with him. He'd taken my hand, and kissed my fingertips, his beautiful brown eyes framed by spiky lashes wet from tears—real tears. I couldn't remember Myles crying a single tear for Jacob, although I knew that he had loved him.

Stephen's tears moved me more than I can find words to express, as did his words.

"I can't bring Jacob back, but someday, I think I'd like to marry you and have a baby with you. Will you think about it?"

If a man had suggested that to me two years earlier, I would have slapped his face and told him to get lost. But time does heal . . . and

I hadn't realized until that moment, that I was strong enough now to want another child.

I smiled through my own tears of gratitude and love. "I'd be overly possessive about him or her," I warned him.

"Me, too, after hearing about what happened to you." He was serious. "But I believe that you have to take risks in life if you want to be happy."

Stephen's belief became my belief.

When I told my parents, I thought they'd be finally happy to see that I'd found someone. Instead, Mom resurrected ugly memories.

"Surely, you're not thinking about getting pregnant again?"

My balloon of happiness burst in a sickening rush of pain and grief. I couldn't believe my mother was reverting back to the days before Jacob.

"Of course, we want children. It's normal and healthy to want children," I added spitefully, wanting to hurt her as she was hurting me. "I'm not the only person ever to lose a child, Mother."

But Mom reminded me of how stubborn she could be. "Maybe not, but it has taken you years to recover, Hilary. You're more fragile than most. Please, honey, don't put yourself through this, again."

I softened a little, realizing that she was truly worried about my mental health. "I'm not going to tempt fate by repeating that old cliché about lightning striking twice. If I have another child and something happens to him or her, I won't hurt any more or less than I did when I lost Jacob. I'm living proof that people do survive."

I swallowed hard, trying not to cry as the grief that was never far away tried to engulf me. And because I loved my mother, I tried to ease her fears. "It doesn't look as if Jessica's going to be giving you another grandchild anytime soon, Mom. Don't you want to be a grandmother?"

"Maybe it will be a girl this time," I heard her mutter before she turned away.

"What?" I asked sharply, but she kept on walking, leaving me alone with my dad, who still suffered from the terrible accident that had taken most of his hearing and my baby's life.

"Dad, aren't you happy for me?"

Dad had blinked at me, clearly in a daze. "What? When did you say you were graduating, honey?"

With a sigh, I turned away. I had yet to tell Jessica. At least, I could pretty much guess her reaction. She had fallen in love with Stephen, too, confessing that I was lucky I had found him first.

Chapter 9

While Jessica and I planned my wedding, I had a weird sense of déjà vu. Mom and I were hardly speaking. We had been having the same old argument, so it was left mostly up to us to make arrangements.

She did attend the wedding, but again, we hardly spoke. I wasn't going to let her spoil my happiness with her crazy fears, so I ignored her for the most part. Afterward, Stephen and I left on a seven-day Alaskan cruise for our honeymoon.

I think I conceived on that cruise, because our beautiful daughter, Candace, was born exactly nine months later. For the first time since Jacob was taken from me, I was holding a baby, again. I think I came close to fainting when the nurse put her into my arms. The experience was both bittersweet and wonderful.

Mom and I made up, and once again, she baffled me by becoming the doting grandmother to a grandchild she hadn't wanted me to have. Jessica and I had just about decided Mom had been suffering from a strange mental illness.

When Candace turned six months old, Stephen and I began working together at the same medical practice. My life was almost perfect again, but this time, I was terrified, constantly waiting for the proverbial "other" shoe to fall. I was married to a man I loved. I had a beautiful daughter, and we were financially stable. We bought a beautiful house on two acres of land.

Each week, Stephen accompanied me along with Candace to put flowers on Jacob's grave. He stood beside me quietly, lending his comfort and his support. He didn't seem to think it was strange that I talked to Jacob, filling him in on our week as if he could hear me and understand. How could a woman not love a man like that?

The proverbial "shoe" did fall, but not in the way I expected. At Candace's first birthday party, I invited Regina and Peter, a couple Stephen and I had met at a convention. We lived within driving distance in different towns, but we got together regularly to have dinner or take in a movie. They had two children, ages three and five. Regina was a realtor, and Peter owned his own landscaping business.

When they arrived, Regina immediately apologized for not calling ahead to tell me they were bringing their nephew, Justin, who was six.

"My sister's going through a messy divorce and needed a break," she explained, pushing Justin forward. "Justin, this is my friend, Hilary. Hilary, this is Justin."

The moment I laid eyes on Justin, I was riveted. Jacob would have been six had he lived, and I knew from memory that his hair would have been the same color, like Justin's. But the startling part was Justin's eyes. They were piercing eyes and slightly rounded—like Mom's and Jessica's. He even had their dimples. In fact, I thought he looked exactly like Jessica's childhood pictures.

I shook my head and blinked back tears, chiding myself for staring and probably scaring the poor kid. Justin wasn't Jacob. It was just a coincidence that he looked like Jessica and Mom to an uncanny degree.

As Stephen took the children into the playroom to fit them with party hats, Regina and I had a moment alone. She stared after Justin, a pitying look in her eyes.

"It's a shame, you know. They adopted him, now they're splitting up. I guess no kid is safe from divorce."

My hands started trembling. I clenched them together, feeling a little dizzy as I said, "Yes, it's a shame. Um, how old is he?"

"Six, this April."

The moisture drained from my mouth as if someone had sucked it dry with one of those horrible suction tubes the dentist used. I knew I was being obsessive and crazy, but I couldn't help myself. Jacob had been born in April.

"Would . . . would you excuse me? I need to get my camera from my bedroom. You can go on in. I don't think any of them bite, but you might want to watch Candace. She's going through that stage." I couldn't believe how calm I sounded, when inside I was shaking like a leaf.

My line of thought was unthinkable. Crazy. Absurd.

But they'd never found a body.

Still . . . I wasn't so crazy I didn't realize I was acting crazy. But that didn't stop me from going into my bedroom, shutting the door, and dragging out one of my old photo albums.

Each and every picture of Jessica made my heart do a funny flip-flop. Justin could have been her twin. I took a deep breath and forced myself to think rationally, to come up with other reasons why Justin would look so much like Jessica.

Jessica had gone to college. It was possible she had sold her eggs, but I couldn't imagine her not telling me about it. We shared every secret, or so I thought, and that sounded like something Jessica would want to explain in great detail.

It sounded like a science fiction movie. But was it any less believable than Jacob actually being alive? My wacky theory unearthed a whole slew of even wackier thoughts. I was being ridiculous, and insane. If Justin was really Jacob, than it meant someone had gone to a lot of

26

trouble to steal him from me. My parents had nearly died in the blast, so it meant that someone was capable of murder.

The bedroom door opened. Stephen poked his handsome head in, flashing me a bright smile. "So that's where you disappeared to." He saw the open photo album in my lap and came on into the room. "Honey, don't you think you picked a strange time to take a trip down memory lane? Our daughter's getting cranky. I think she might have to miss her own party in lieu of a nap."

He came closer, peering over my shoulder to the open photo album. "Hey, that looks like that kid Regina and Peter brought over."

From a distance, I heard myself say, "It's Jessica when she was young."

"That kid . . . what's his name?"

"Justin," I whispered, but Stephen didn't notice.

"He could be Jessica's twin."

"Just a coincidence," I whispered, more to convince myself than to convince Stephen. Stephen didn't have a clue as to where my crazy thoughts were going. "Just a bizarre coincidence."

"Hilary? Are you okay? You look as white as a ghost."

I almost laughed at his uncanny choice of words. "Actually, I think I might be going a little nuts. Will you still love me?" He completely missed the underlying seriousness of my tone.

"Of course." He kissed the top of my head. "Let's get back to our daughter's party."

But I couldn't concentrate on the party, or my daughter, for that matter. I zeroed in on Regina and pulled her aside, drilling her with more questions about Justin.

"How old was he when your sister got him?"

She shot me a puzzled look. "About six weeks old. Why?"

I ignored her question. "Did you get to see him right away?"

"Well, yeah, like the next day. April was so excited, she called the entire family in as if she'd given birth. Why?"

Knowing I'd have to give her an explanation soon, I shot the questions at her. "Do you remember if he had a scratch on his cheek?"

By this time, Regina was frowning. "A scratch? You expect me to remember if he had a scratch on his cheek? Hilary, what's wrong? Why are you asking me all of these questions?"

"I'll explain in a minute. Did April take his picture right after she got him?"

Regina laughed as if I'd asked a silly question. "The very next day, in fact. Paid a bundle for professional pictures."

"Do you have one?"

"As a matter of fact, I do." She took out her wallet and thumbed through wallet-sized pictures of her kids, nieces, and nephews. She extracted one and handed it to me. "Wasn't he an angel? She was so lucky to get such a pretty baby. I figure one of his parents had to be a looker."

I stared at the picture. It blurred before my eyes. I blinked rapidly, then again, seriously wondering if I was having a breakdown after all these years.

It couldn't possibly be.

But it was.

It was a picture of my baby, right down to the scratch on his cheek, a scratch he'd given himself trying to suck on his fist, alerting me that his nails needed to be trimmed.

The picture began to blur, again. Blackness began to encroach upon my peripheral vision, until there was nothing but a tiny pinpoint of light in the center. I felt myself crumple. I knew that I was fainting, even heard my husband exclaim in surprise, then everything went silent.

Chapter 10

When I came to, Stephen was hovering over me, his face lined with concern. I bolted upright. "Where's Justin?"

Stephen gently pushed me back down. "They left. Regina didn't want to upset you further. She said Justin must remind you of the child you lost."

I grabbed Stephen's hand and squeezed so hard, he winced. I'm sure my eyes were burning with a crazy light. "He doesn't just resembled Jacob, Stephen. He is Jacob! I saw his baby picture. There . . . there was a scratch on his cheek, just like the scratch on Jacob's cheek the last time I saw him—in the exact same place! His nails needed cutting, but I was always afraid I'd cut his finger or something." Agitated, I thrust back my hair and tried to get up again.

And again, Stephen pushed me back down. "Calm down, honey." He hesitated, then said, "You know that kid can't be Jacob, don't you?"

I started to argue, but instinct warned me I'd wind up on the psycho ward if I continued insisting that Jacob was alive. Stephen loved me enough to commit me. I feigned a confused look, but not the deep shudder that rippled over me.

My baby was alive! But how? Why? Questions I couldn't answer, yet, but I intended to find the answers. Oh, yeah. "Good grief. I guess I was more stressed out over this party than I thought! I hate it that Regina felt she had to leave after driving all that way," I said to Stephen.

"She understood."

Understood? Or was she hiding something? At that moment, nearly everyone I knew was suspect—with the exception of Stephen, who hadn't known me before Jacob.

I'm ashamed to say that later, I couldn't remember a single moment about my daughter's party. Thankfully, Stephen videotaped a good deal of it. He also captured Justin on film for few heart-stopping seconds before I fainted.

In the middle of the night, I got out of bed and crept into the living room, watching that fleeting view of Justin—Jacob—again and again. Finally, I gave in to the sobs burning my chest, crying as quietly as I could. In the midst of my bewilderment and grief, a terrible anger gathered.

Someone had taken Jacob from me, and it hadn't been God. Not only did I owe Him about a hundred apologies, I had a lot of detective work ahead of me. It wouldn't be easy keeping Stephen in the dark, but I knew that I had to try or risk being hauled to a doctor and put on medication, or even worse, admitted to the psychiatric hospital.

There was one person, however, that I knew I could count on, and even that would take some powerful persuading. Jessica loved me, but could I convince her of the truth? More importantly, could I convince her not to freak out and go to Stephen before I could gather evidence?

The next day, I packed up Candace and drove to the city, calling Jessica on my cell phone along the way. I didn't want to give her a chance to make excuses for not having lunch with me.

Three hours later, she and I sat in a restaurant, feeding Candace crackers and pizza crust to keep her busy. Jessica listened to my wild story without interruption, her eyes growing bigger by the moment. When I finished, she sat back and stared at me long and hard.

"You're not having a breakdown, are you? You really believe Jacob is still alive."

Tempering my excitement, I lifted a questioning brow. "You sound as if you'd rather I was having the breakdown. Listen, Jessica, you've never known me to jump to conclusions, have you?"

Reluctantly, Jessica shook her head. "But Hilary, you have a death certificate on Jacob."

"They never found his body, not a trace of it."

"Okay. How about this: Can you think of one single reason anyone would want to fake your baby's death, then steal him from you? You have to admit–being the reasonably intelligent woman that you are–it's more than a little far-fetched."

She had me there, but I wasn't deterred. "No, I can't think of a motive. That doesn't mean there isn't a motive, does it? If I can prove that Justin is Jacob, then they'll have to launch an investigation, won't they?" I dodged a flying piece of soggy pizza crust that Candace gleefully threw at me and clasped Jessica's hand, unable to contain my excitement.

"Sis, you have to swear to me that you won't say a word of this to anyone. If Regina's sister gets wind of this, she might take Justin and run."

"I'm not certain I'd blame her," Jessica said, honestly. "She's raised him for six years."

My voice was harsh as I reminded her. "Maybe so, but he's my baby! Just because she might not know anything about this doesn't give her the right to keep him!"

Jessica shook her head, looking dazed. But I could tell she was beginning to believe me, or at least give me the benefit of a doubt.

"I don't know, Hilary. If by some miracle you're right about this, the trail is already six years old. Don't get your hopes up that anyone can find out what happened."

"Haven't you ever watched the television show that's about old, unsolved police cases?"

"Have you had a CAT scan done of your brain, lately?"

I made a face at her. "Very funny. Are you in or out?"

She let out a lusty sigh that said she wasn't exactly thrilled about the entire idea. "I guess I'm in. I can't let you race around playing amateur detective without me. How can I help?"

I bit my lip, realizing I didn't know where to start. "Um, I need more evidence than just the picture and my word. I need Jacob's DNA to compare against Justin's, but the fire pretty much took care of that happening."

"Not necessarily," Jessica said slowly. "I never told you because I didn't want to make you sad, but I still have a pacifier he used that you left at my house, and a sleeper he'd spit up on. I tucked them both away in a back drawer, thinking there might come a time when it would be appropriate to give them to you."

My eyes misted. I tried not to be angry, because Jessica may very well have solved the case single-handedly.

"If you knew how badly I wanted to have something of his . . . never mind. Just thank God you kept them. You didn't wash the sleeper?"

Jessica shook her head, her own eyes bright with a sheen of tears. "I couldn't bear to look at them that long. I just put them in a plastic bag and put them away."

"You're an angel," I said, fervently. "And the best sister a girl could have."

She feigned a scowl. "It's about time you realized that. So what's next? Won't you have to have something from Justin? A hair sample, blood sample, something like that? And won't you have to have some type of authorization to get a DNA test?"

Leave it to my sister to raise the toughest questions, I thought. "I'll cross that bridge when I come to it. Meanwhile, I already have an idea on how to get a DNA sample from Justin."

When I didn't immediately tell her, she leaned close. "Are you going to share? We're in this together, remember?"

I hesitated, knowing I would have a battle on my hands when I told her what I had planned, especially her part in it. And I was right. She gawked at me as if I'd lost my mind. Maybe I had.

"You're planning to march right into their home and cut off a lock of his hair? And I'm supposed to distract the mother by needing to change Candace's diaper."

"Exactly. April will have to show you to the bedroom where you can change her."

"And you think this kid—"

"Jacob . . . . Justin."

"Justin . . . will just stand there and let you take out a pair of scissors and cut his hair?"

"He will if I convince him he has gum in his hair, and that he'll get into trouble if I don't quickly get it out." I wasn't at all sure of myself, but I refused to let it get me down. "He's six, Jessica. They'll believe anything at that age. Look what you convinced me to do at that age."

"True, true." She frowned as if something had just occurred to her. "What if April knows about your reaction, and won't let us in the house? What if she thinks you're a nut case?"

"If that happens, we'll have to go to plan B."

"And that would be?"

"I haven't thought of it, yet. Anyway, I don't think Regina told her. She's very protective of April, and April's going through a rough time right now. To be on the safe side, however, I'm going to give Regina a call and apologize for my silly reaction. Convince her that it was a shock to see a kid look so much like the baby I lost."

"Good thinking . . . if she hasn't already told her sister about the incident. And our reason for visiting this April?"

"We couldn't find Regina at home, and we thought she might be at April's."

"Sounds like you've got it all figured out."

I took a deep breath and tried to smile. "I think I do."

"I still think you're taking a risk."

"Got any better ideas?" I challenged, then ruined it by sounding hopeful. "Don't you see, sis, that I can't wait around for a better idea? Now that I know Jacob's alive, it's eating me up inside not being with him. He's my baby, my firstborn. I thought he was dead."

Chapter 11

I will believe to my dying moment that God was on my side that day. April was a little flustered to see us . . . having met just once before when she stopped by with Regina after shopping. She was too polite not to invite us in.

Trembling with anticipation at seeing Justin/Jacob again, I offered her an overly bright smile and set our plan in motion. "Oh, we can't stay, but I wouldn't mind changing Candace while we're here. I don't think she'll make it home with this dirty diaper."

April looked horrified at the thought of me making Candace wait. "Of course, come right in! You can change her in the bedroom. I'll show you."

Tearing my hungry gaze from the little boy sitting in the floor in front of the television, I transferred Candace to Jessica's arms, more than a little smug at the flash of shock on my sister's face at seeing Justin.

"Do you mind, sis? My back is killing me." Without waiting for an answer, I hooked the small diaper bag over her shoulder. "She always lies still for you better, anyway."

The unsuspecting April laughed at that. "Isn't that how they all do? The bedroom's this way."

She waved a hand in Justin's direction before leading Jessica from the room. "Justin, say hi to Hilary. You went to her house a few days ago, remember?" When he didn't appear to hear her, she shook her head and rolled her eyes. "He's like a statue when he's watching television. You'd have to knock him on the head to get his attention."

April wasn't kidding. The moment they were out of sight, I took out my scissors and silently approached Justin. I had the lock of hair clenched in my fist and my scissors back in my purse, before he even realized I was behind him.

When he jerked around and stared at me with his big eyes, I had to lock my knees in place to keep from crumbling to the floor and gathering him into my arms.

He might have been six, but there wasn't anything childish about the suspicion that lit his eyes at the sight of me standing that close to him, wearing an undoubtedly yearning expression.

"You're that lady who got sick at the party," he said, still eyeing me suspiciously. "Are you still sick?"

I shook my head. I wasn't able to speak around the great big lump in my throat.

33

Ten minutes later, we were back in my minivan. Jessica belted Candace into her car seat while I sat like a wax dummy, staring through the windshield. I was still clutching the lock of hair in my hand. Suddenly, I wanted to roll down the window and throw it into the wind. What if I was wrong, after getting my hopes up? What if Justin wasn't Jacob, and I truly was suffering from delusions?

And then, Hilary slid into the passenger seat and drew her belt across her lap. "That was, without a doubt, the strangest moment I've ever had. You were right, Hilary, about one thing. He looks exactly like me when I was a kid. That, and the fact that he was adopted, and his birthday is in April keeps me in the game."

"It isn't a game."

Jessica blew out an irritated sigh. "You know what I mean. God. I feel as if someone dropped me into the middle of a made-for-television movie."

"A lot of those movies are based on true stories, Jessica." Carefully, I unfolded my fingers, staring down at the hair stuck to my sweaty palm. "Can you get me that sandwich bag out of the glove compartment?"

She brought it out and helped me carefully transfer the hair to the plastic sack. I stuck it into my purse and started the car. "Now, to convince someone to run a DNA test."

"I think we should go straight to the D.A.'s office. A friend of mine from college works in the mailroom. He might be able to get us an appointment, or at least hook us up with someone who can. Swing by my place, and we'll pick up Jacob's pacifier and the sleeper."

Two hours later, I was making a mental note to send Jessica's old college friend, Addison, a nice gift basket as we crowded into the elevator after talking to the D. A. Candace had fallen asleep in her carrier, and my arm ached from holding it.

"I can't believe it was that easy," I said, shock lingering in my voice.

Jessica grinned at my expression. "It's election year."

"Thank-you God," I murmured sincerely. "All we have to do is wait two weeks for the results."

Without a doubt, I knew it would be the longest two weeks of my life.

I spent plenty of time in those two weeks waiting on the DNA test, asking myself the same questions again and again. Who would do this? Why would they do it? If a ruthless couple wanted a baby that badly, they could have stolen him any number of times without blowing up my house and nearly killing my parents.

Yet for some unfathomable reason, they had wanted everyone to believe he was dead. Why? Who?

My husband and I were very close, so it wasn't surprising that he noticed that I was distracted and anxious.

"Something's bothering you," he said one night. He must have noticed I just picked at my food. "Are you going to share?"

Believe me, I felt really guilty as I said, "Just PMS, honey. You know I always get a little edgy." Stephen was my life, but I just couldn't trust him to believe me at this point. Now, if the DNA confirmed that Justin and Jacob were one and the same child, then I would have something to back me up when I related the horrendous facts to him.

"Hmm," he said, clearly not convinced. He stared hard at me for a long, uncomfortable moment. "You know you can talk to me about anything, Hilary."

I smiled at that. "Are you practicing being a father of a teenager?" But even my attempt to lighten the mood and change the dangerous subject reminded me of Jacob. When Jacob came to live with us, he'd be closer to being a teenager than he would be to Candace's age.

"Are we going to have another baby?" Stephen asked.

I dropped my gaze quickly, lest he see the excitement and anticipation in my eyes. "No, no. I'm not pregnant. We agreed to wait a few years before having another baby, so I wouldn't make a decision like that without talking it over with you." It was the truth.

"You're hiding something," he said, sounding hurt. "I can tell."

For one insane moment, I considered blurting out the story to him and taking my chances. Then I smartened up. I couldn't investigate from a padded room or zoned out on pills.

"Really, Stephen. Nothing's wrong, and I'm not hiding anything."

"Okay. If you say so." We ate in silence for a few moments before he changed the subject, much to my relief. "I saw a new patient today. Looks like he might be schizophrenic."

"Really?" I replied, absently. I was thinking about how Jacob would react to finding out he had a little sister.

"Yeah, really. His family is really worried about him. They said he's been distracted, staring off into space as if listening to something only he can hear. Almost as if he's hiding something."

My relief was short-lived as I realized what Stephen was getting at. He wasn't always direct, but he got his point across. I gave up the pretense of eating as I got to my feet.

"I need to wake Candace from her nap or I'll never get her to sleep tonight."

"Running away won't solve anything," Stephen called after me, sounding frustrated.

I should have stayed and convinced him, but the truth was I hated lying to my husband. Maybe I was wrong not to trust him, but I just

35

couldn't take that chance. He knew my history, knew how long it had taken me to get over losing my baby. No, I couldn't take that chance, not yet.

Picking up my sleeping daughter from her crib, I cuddled her against my chest. "You're going to have a new brother," I whispered. Then I froze. Hearing myself saying the fantastical words out loud, frightened me.

I truly did sound disturbed. Was I? Was I actually suffering a nervous breakdown and didn't know it? Recalling Jessica's shocked expression on seeing Justin, eased my mind. If Jessica thought I was losing my mind, she wouldn't play along. She would go straight to Stephen.

Chapter 12

For the last few days of waiting, I did my best to act normal around Stephen. It wasn't easy, since we worked together at the same clinic.

The call from the district attorney's office came while I was in between patients. I snatched up the phone, my heart pounding with anticipation and terror. I knew there was a chance that I could be wrong. Many might say there was more than a chance.

"Mrs. Magadan . . . I have some disturbing news." The southern twang in the district attorney's voice was more pronounced. "Maybe it would be better if you and your husband came into my office."

The first time I tried to speak, it came out a whisper. I had to clear my throat several times.

"My husband isn't the one. I mean, he isn't my son's father, so I haven't told him about my suspicions. I wanted to be sure before I did." Hint, hint. "Could—could you at least tell me if the DNA matched?"

The silence that followed was like one of those strange dreams where you're trying to run and seem to be moving in slow motion. A moment felt like an hour.

Finally, he spoke. "I have to warn you, Mrs. Magadan, that you can't take any action to regain your son pending an investigation."

My heart dropped to my stomach and soared into my throat. I had to swallow it back down. "The DNA matched? It matched? Justin is Jacob?" I didn't realize until that moment how much I had doubted my own sanity. "Oh my God! It's true?"

I was practically screaming into the phone. My office door burst open. Tasha, the receptionist, stood in the doorway. She looked wildly around the room. Stephen came running in behind her.

"What is it? Hilary? What is it?" Then he saw that I was on the phone, and my face must have blanched of all color. He hurried around the desk to me and tried to take the phone. "Is it Candace? Is she hurt?"

The phone might as well have been cemented to my hand, because he wasn't budging it. Faintly, I heard myself say in an almost normal tone, "Tomorrow morning's fine. Yes, thank-you."

Two pairs of anxious eyes drilled holes in me as I hung up the phone. I avoided looking at Stephen; afraid I'd break down if I did.

"It's okay, Tasha. You can leave us alone, now. Everything's fine." More than fine. It was great. Bizarre, but great. A miracle.

"You wanna tell me what the heck is going on? You just scared ten years off my life!" Stephen sounded angry, but I knew it was due to worry.

Finally, I looked at him, took a deep, shuddering breath, and just blurted it out. "Jacob's alive, Stephen. That was the district attorney's office. He said their DNA matched."

Stephen gave his head a bewildered shake. "Back up. Whose DNA matched?"

"Justin's and Jacob's. Justin is Jacob, the baby that I believed died in the house explosion."

As if his legs had suddenly gone weak, Stephen stumbled to the couch and sat hard. "How did you get a DNA test? I thought you said there wasn't a trace of Jacob left because of the blast and the intensity of the fire."

I nodded. "That's right, but Jessica, bless her heart, kept a pacifier and a jumpsuit he'd worn that I left at her house. She never told me because she didn't want to upset me."

"That explains how you got Jacob's DNA, but now how you got Justin's. I can't believe they just agreed to let you test him."

Flushing in remembrance, I told Stephen what Jessica and I had done to get Justin's hair sample. In the telling, it sounded like the hair-brained idea of someone mentally ill.

"So you confided in Jessica, but not in me?"

His obvious hurt didn't come as a surprise, but I was ready with an explanation.

"Honestly, Stephen, if I had kept insisting that Justin was Jacob, would you have believed me? Even I admit that the entire idea sounds impossible. It means that someone deliberately blew up my house and stole Jacob from me, meaning for me to think he was dead and risking killing my parents."

"You're right, it does sound bizarre. Straight out of a thriller movie." He jumped to his feet and came to me, his eyes wide with shock. "God, Hilary! This is . . . is . . . ."

When he kept floundering for the right words, I laughed and rose to walk into his embrace. The tears came fast and hot, soaking his shirt. But I was smiling.

"I know I should be furious and asking myself why, but all I can think about is that Jacob isn't dead. I feel like a miracle has happened."

He soothed me by rubbing my back. I could hear the smile in his voice. "It is a miracle, honey. You can bet the bank on that."

"I can't wait to tell my parents—and Candace! Candace has a brother and my parents have another grandchild."

"Yes, she does."

Sleeping that night was asking a little much, so I didn't mind lying awake, thinking and remembering, anticipating seeing Jacob again. But just before dawn, darker thoughts intruded. A woman who obviously loved Jacob, raised him as Justin. What would this do to his adolescent mind when he found out I was his mother, not April? What if he didn't want to come home with us, when the time came?

Eventually, knowing I'd never go to sleep, I made a pot of coffee and sat in the dim kitchen, attempting to put together an impossible puzzle. I still couldn't imagine that someone had gone to such drastic lengths to steal Jacob.

Had April and her husband paid a lot of money for him? Had he been a black-market baby, and had there really been an actual black market these days?

Had April or her husband known anything at all, or were they innocent victims, as Jacob had been? Hopefully, the district attorney would be able to answer some of my questions.

Dex McFarlane was a middle-aged, fit man with blond hair, mustache, and a receding hairline. He had a presence, however, that made him seem taller than he actually was.

"I have to admit, this one is a new one on me," he told us after we were seated in his office. "You're both physician's assistants?"

"Yes," I answered nervously. Did he know how hard it was for me to sit in his office shooting the breeze when I could be getting to know my son? Stephen, sensing my impatience, squeezed my hand, and took the initiative.

"Where do we go from here?" he asked.

Dex shook his head, clearly baffled. "Truthfully, I'm not sure. If the couple who adopted him have valid papers and a birth certificate, then we'll have to go back even further."

Tears burned the backs of my eyes. I twisted my hands around Stephen's. "Can–can we at least have him back while the investigation is ongoing? I mean, you know, he's my son."

The district attorney studied the far wall, frowning. Slowly, he said, "I think we'll have to start with you, Mrs. Magadan. Frankly, I don't know you from Adam. You could be making up this whole thing, for all I know."

"Why would I do that?" I exclaimed, my voice rising.

He shrugged. "Stranger things have happened. Like I said, let's verify your background and the facts as you've laid them out to me. Then we'll go from there."

With extreme effort, I swallowed my humiliation. "You'll find everything will check out, Mr. McFarlane."

He shot me a stern, hard look. "For your sake, I hope it does, Mrs. Magadan. In the meantime, sit tight, okay? My secretary will give you the required papers to fill out so we can make the necessary calls. She'll need to get copies of your driver's license, birth certificate, and things like that. Do you have a copy of your son's birth certificate?"

I shook my head. "It burned in the fire, and I didn't see any reason to file for another one. All I have is a death certificate."

"She'll need a copy of that, too, and a copy of the fire chef's report. You could speed things along by making it easy for her to have that information."

"I'll get her that fire report." Anything at all that would speed up the time when I could see my son again, hold him close. And bring him home, where he belonged.

"Good. Give me a call next week and I'll bring you up to date."

We were dismissed, but I left with a bounce in my stride. His threat to investigate me was a little humiliating, but I knew that he would find that everything I had told him was the truth.

The moment we were in the car, I turned to Stephen. "Do you think you can get the pool ready by this weekend?"

Stephen's brows rose. "It's only the middle of April. Do you think it's warm enough to swim?"

"I think it is. It's been in the upper eighties the last few days. I want to have a pool party and invite Regina and Peter . . . and April and Jacob."

"Justin," Stephen corrected, tapping me on the nose. "If you don't want to blow everything, you'd better call him Justin." Concern crept into his eyes. "Honey, do you think this is a good idea? To be around your son all day and not be able to claim him?" He shook his head. "I still can't believe it."

"Believe it," I said. "Jacob is alive and well, and someone's going to pay for the hell they put me through."

"Now that's an honest, healthy reaction. I was beginning to get worried about your lack of anger."

"Oh, it's there. Believe me, it's there. I can't stand not seeing him, Stephen, now that I know for certain." I pulled out my cell phone and turned it on. "I've got to call Jessica. She's going to scream."

"That's an understatement," Stephen said with a chuckle.

At Stephen's suggestion, I took a day or two a week off from work. I nearly ran myself ragged during the four days before the scheduled party. I bought a new swimsuit for Candace and myself. I created a menu that would be appealing to a six-year-old boy.

When I called Regina to tell her about the pool party, I tried to smooth over the troubling memory of birthday party. At first, she was reluctant, and I nearly panicked.

"I don't know if it's such a good idea inviting April and Justin," she said hesitantly.

I could tell she was trying to tread softly to keep from upsetting me again. Crossing my fingers as I told the lie.

"As a matter of fact, Stephen thinks it's the best idea I've had in a long while. He said that being around someone like Justin, who looks so much like I picture Jacob looking had he lived, is a positive step in grounding myself to reality."

"Really?"

"Really." I laughed. "Anyway, you don't have to worry. I won't be freaking out on you or anything. I promise. Besides, I want the chance to make it up to Justin. He had to leave before cake and ice cream."

Regina relaxed, chuckling as she said, "Yeah, he sulked all the way home."

"So you're okay with it?" I held my breath and closed my eyes, praying hard.

"Well, yeah. I'm okay with it. I never mentioned the episode to April. She would have freaked."

When I got off the phone, I swung Candace up in a joyful dance around the living room. "We're going to see your big brother again, sweetie!"

Candace made happy sounds when I swung her around again.

The day of the party I was so wired, I broke one of my own rules about taking drugs, and I took an allergy medicine pill so that I could calm down. Otherwise, I think I would have jittered apart at the seams.

When Regina and her family arrived, I could barely contain my excitement. Imagine my extreme disappointment when Regina told me that April and Justin wouldn't be coming.

She sounded exasperated with her sister. "She doesn't realize how overprotective she's being, and how it's affecting Justin."

I somehow managed to sound normal as I said, "I didn't realize she was overprotective."

"Well, to give her credit, I guess I can't blame her." She looked around to make certain we were alone, and lowered her voice. "I mean, if one of my kids had hemophilia, then I guess I'd be paranoid, too."

"Oh." It was all I could muster. Inside, I was a shaking mess of shock and fear for the son I'd just found.

"She's afraid to let him do any of the normal things most boys do, like swimming. I brought him to the party without telling her, knowing she'd make a fuss. I was hoping to add a little sunshine to his life, you know? I mean, he's on medication constantly, and she and I have taken a class at the hospital, so we'll know what to do if he injures himself, or has a nosebleed."

My mouth was dry as I asked, "Is it that serious?"

Regina nodded solemnly. "Yes, it is. He has the worst kind. It's usually inherited from the mother, but you probably already knew that."

I was familiar with the term and remembered a little about the disease, but not enough. I wanted to call off the party and hop on the Internet to refresh my memory. Like most people, I had only retained the information I thought I would need.

"Hilary? You look a little pale. You're not about to faint on me again, are you?"

I couldn't make any promises, but I was going to try my best not to faint, or make her suspicious in any way. Which meant the party had to continue, despite the shock she'd given me.

Later that night after our happy, yet exhausted guests had gone home and Candace was down for the night, I was reminded of why I loved Stephen so much. Just when I was starting to have doubts, he knew exactly what to say to shore them up.

He tapped the computer screen in front of me. "Look, honey, it says here that sometimes the person who has hemophilia created the gene. It isn't always inherited."

"Most of the time it is." I wanted to believe him, I really did. "Maybe Mom's a carrier and we just never knew it, and I'm a carrier and that's how Jacob got the disease."

"According to our research, you could be right. Why don't you ask your mom, just in case? She might know about it . . . that might be why she didn't want you to have a boy. Mothers who are carriers usually pass it on to the boy, who actually has the disease."

He massaged my tense shoulders, his voice soothing. "Honey, DNA doesn't lie. Justin is Jacob. I don't know where the hemophilia came from, but it doesn't mean that he isn't yours."

"Still . . . it's strange. I don't know anyone in our family that suffered from it." My eyes filled with tears as I added, "And I hate the thought that I could be a carrier, and that I could have given it to Justin. Regina says he's miserable, that April won't let him do hardly anything."

"Well, that will soon change, won't it? He'll be coming to live with us."

"What makes you think I won't be the same way? After losing him once—"

Stephen crushed his mouth to mine, halting my words. He raised his head and looked deeply into my eyes. "Honey, you are the best mother in the world. I don't care how crazy with worry you'd be, you wouldn't make your child miserable."

"Will you come with me tomorrow when I tell my parents?"

"Of course." He flashed me a mischievous grin. "I wouldn't miss it for the world. Make it late, so I can be there. You know how it gets at work; there's always an emergency or something that holds us up."

Chapter 13

Dad's reaction to the news didn't surprise me; he looked confused. Mom's reaction, however, stunned me. She turned a pale white, then red. I was immediately concerned that she might be on the verge of having a heart attack.

I knelt before her chair, hoping to calm her and check her pulse at the same time. It was erratic, but strong. "Mom? Are you okay? You look like you've seen a ghost. I know it's a shock, but it's great news, isn't it?"

She recovered slowly, but her color remained high. "How could he have survived the blast, Hilary? I was there . . . I saw the devastation. It nearly killed your father, and he was found near the door."

"You told me to stay in the living room so I could hear Jacob if he woke up," Dad piped in, "but I thought I heard you come back, so I went to the door to look."

None of us took him seriously. More and more, his mind was slipping away from us. He had his lucid moments, but it was hard to tell what was actually real or in his imagination. Anger surged through me. Someone had done this to my dad so they could steal Jacob from me.

I pulled a chair close to hers and quietly told her how I'd found out about Justin, and how Jessica and I had proven our suspicions.

Her faint smile held a hint of irony and something else I couldn't define. "Well, you and your sister always were clever, especially when you put your heads together."

I shot a questioning glance at Stephen, who nodded his assurance. "Mom, I found out that Jacob is a hemophiliac. Does anyone in our family have this disease, or is anyone you know a carrier?"

She jerked her head back, her face blanching white again. Her reaction puzzled me. I was further confused.

"Of course not," she snapped. "You would know something like that."

I wanted to call her a liar, but the respect that had been drilled into me, prevented the words from leaving my mouth. Instead, I turned to Dad. It was probably useless to ask him, but his long-term memory was better than his short term, I reminded myself.

"Dad? How about your side of the family?"

Dad blinked at me. "What?"

I slowly repeated my question, silently urging him to pay attention. He frowned down at the remote in his hand, and then scratched his head. "Hemophilia? The only person I've ever known with that disease is Dr. Bernard. I filled his prescription every month for twenty years."

Mom made a strange, gasping noise, and then began coughing. I had to pat her on the back several times before she could catch her breath. When she recovered, Dad spoke again, his voice quivering with confusion.

"Evette . . . did I work yesterday? I can't remember."

Mom's voice was whiplash sharp as she said, "No, Wesley, you didn't. You haven't worked in six years."

"Then who's filling Dr. Bernard's medicine? He has to have that clotting agent, you know. If he cuts himself, he could bleed to death."

"We sold the business, Wesley. Go into the kitchen and fix yourself a sandwich. You're just confusing everyone with your rambling."

It was on the tip of my tongue to point out to Mom that maybe she was being a little hard on Dad, but one look at her tightly lined mouth stalled the words. Dad obediently got up and left the room.

With a hand that trembled, she pushed her hair from her forehead. Her shaky smile looked forced. "It gets tedious sometimes, day in and day out. Sometimes he's my husband, and other times he's a stranger." She put a gentle hand on top of my head, and then let it drop. "Now, tell me more. Who's the woman that has Jacob?"

By the time we left, Mom was her old self again. She even began to sound excited at the prospect of seeing Jacob again, although the lingering shock in her eyes worried me.

In the car, I put a stalling hand on Stephen's as he went for the key. "Wait. Maybe we should stay a bit longer. Mom looked really shaken."

"Can you blame her? That was a pretty wild story we just told her."

"Yeah, I know." I frowned, biting my lip. "I guess this means that Jacob just developed hemophilia on his own, since no one in our family has it. I already talked to Myles's mom, and there's no history in her family."

"They could still be carriers and not know it," Stephen pointed out. "Even you."

"Then I should get tested," I decided. "Since female carriers are the only ones that can give it to the male children, if I'm not a carrier, then he couldn't have gotten it from me. I think I'd feel better knowing."

"In that case, you should go to Dr. Bernard. If your dad's right and he has it, then we could ask him some questions. He should be an expert in the field."

"Good idea."

I called Dr. Bernard's office when we got home and persuaded the receptionist to work me in the following day, using my previous employment with him and his friendship with my parents as leverage.

That night, I talked to Jessica and brought her up-to-date. She insisted on going with me to see Dr. Bernard since Stephen had a full schedule at the clinic and couldn't take off another day.

Dr. Bernard had aged some, but he was one of those men who aged well. He seemed pleased to see me, enveloping me in a bear hug that nearly squeezed the breath out of my lungs.

Keeping an arm around my shoulder, he beamed at me. "You're looking well, Hilary. How are things going in your life? How's work?"

"Things are going great. Candace just turned one recently, and I found out that Jacob's still alive." Jessica gave my arm a sharp pinch and leaned forward to whisper in my ear.

"You could have eased into that one, Hilary. He's not as young as he looks."

Dr. Bernard looked at me blankly for a moment. Then his eyes widened in shock. "Did you saw Jacob is still alive?" He sat forward abruptly, looking from Jessica, to me, then back to Jessica. I saw the silent question in his eyes when he looked at my sister.

"No, I'm not crazy, Dr. Bernard. Jacob really is alive. Apparently, there was an elaborate plot to steal him from me."

"Amazing! I can't believe it! Have you found the people responsible? Do you have him back with you now?"

"No, we haven't, and no, we don't. But soon, he'll be home." I shifted, unwilling to dwell too long on a subject that kept me up at nights: that of getting Jacob back home. "I'm here because Dad told me you were a hemophiliac. I hope you don't mind that he told me, he's not in his right mind, you know."

Dr. Bernard flushed a dull red. His eyes hardened a fraction. "Lucky for him, or I'd have to be upset at the breach in confidentiality. I don't like people knowing my private business."

His hardened expression made me squirm. I felt compelled to take up for Dad. "Like I said . . . he can't help himself, and I apologize on his behalf."

He picked up a message pad and tapped it against the desk. "Apology accepted. Now, what can I do for you?"

"Well . . . I want to get tested. We just found out that Jacob is a hemophiliac, and I want to see if I'm a carrier."

"That's unlikely. In any case, you'll have to go to someone who specializes in genetics to get tested. I'm afraid I'm just a small-town doctor. We don't have that type of equipment."

I sat there in shock for a moment. Dr. Bernard had suddenly become cold and unfriendly, and I couldn't fathom why. Was he that upset that Dad had told me about his disease? And why would he be ashamed? It wasn't a disease that evoked shame, was it? I felt frustrated because I knew so little about it.

"Come on, sis, let's go." Jessica tugged at me arm, pulling me to my feet. She shot Dr. Bernard a shame-shame look. "Thanks for your help," she said, sarcastically.

"Anytime," Dr. Bernard said, but didn't sound as if he meant it.

In the car, Jessica said, "That was a strange meeting."

"Yeah. I don't think he was too happy about Dad blabbing his mouth about his condition." I started the van and pulled onto the road, merging into traffic. "You don't mind if we swing by April's house since we're in the neighborhood? Maybe I can catch a glimpse of him playing outside." My heart ached with the need to see him again, to assure myself that he was alive and well.

"Neighborhood?" Jessica laughed. "April's is sixty miles out of our way, sis. And from what you've told me about April's paranoia, it isn't likely you'll catch him outside playing."

"Still . . . if you don't mind?" Pleading with Jessica normally did the trick, and today was no exception.

"Why the hell not? I'd like to see him again, myself."

Later, I could have kissed the guardian angel on my shoulder for nudging me in that direction on that particular day.

Chapter 14

As we turned down the quiet, suburban street where Jacob lived, I had a strange sense of urgency, as if something were about to happen. I shook it off.

"Look's like they might be gone," Jessica commented as we cruised by April's tidy brick house.

I was about to agree when I noticed something different. I hit my brakes, throwing Jessica the length of her seat belt. She glared at me.

"What the hell? Hilary, you nearly gave me whiplash!"

"Shh! Look. In the backyard." I pointed to a section of yard on the side of the house that led straight into the backyard. "The last time we were here, there was a swing set."

"You should have been a cop," Jessica muttered, following my finger. "Because I don't remember a swing set. What are you getting at?"

I shot her an impatient look. "It's not there, anymore." I backed up the van and studied the front yard, then the front of the house. Finally I checked out the garage. April's car was there, a shiny dark green.

A chill raced down my spine. "She's moving," I stated with absolute conviction.

"What?" Jessica stared at me as if I'd lost my mind. "Just because they took down the swing set doesn't mean they're moving!"

"It isn't just the swing set. There was a barbecue grill, one of those fancy ones, in the garage. It's gone. There was also a woman's bicycle. And look—" I pointed to the car. "There are boxes piled in the backseat, and a lamp."

Jessica peered through the window. Finally, she rolled it down and stuck her head out, shading her eyes against the bright sun.

"You're right. She's moving. Either it's a coincidence, or someone tipped her off."

With a squall of tires, I pulled my van in behind the car. If April wanted to leave, she'd have to go through my minivan, first.

Silently, Jessica and I got out of the van and went to the front door. I knocked and waited, seething inside, terrified that she had come so close to taking Jacob from me. Terrified that she might have used another vehicle and was already gone with him.

When no one came to the door, I beat on it harder, shouting at the top of my lungs, "April! I know you're in there! You'd better let me in, or I'm going to call the cops! He's my son!"

The door opened abruptly. A white-faced April stood on the threshold. "Leave us alone," she said coldly. "He's my son. I've raised him, taken care of him when he was sick . . ." She broke down and began to sob. "You have a child! Why can't you just let me have Justin?"

I squashed the pang of pity I felt for her and stormed by her into the house. Jessica followed. My gaze roamed the room, filled with boxes, looking for Jacob. He wasn't in sight. Panic seized my gut, wrenching it painfully.

"Where is he? How did you find out? Did they send someone to question you?" I would have been surprised if they had, since I had yet to hear from the district attorney's office about their investigation on myself.

"He's—he's in his room, but wait!" She dared to grab my arm to keep me from moving in that direction. "Don't do this. Don't scare him. He doesn't know anything."

I felt frigid inside. I was ready to punch anyone who stood in my way. My voice dripped with ice as I said with deceptive softness, "Do you have any idea what you're into? You'll be charged with kidnapping, attempted murder—"

Her shocked gasp caught my attention.

I felt a scary kind of glee at her horrified expression. "Yes, attempted murder. Whoever is responsible for taking Jacob nearly killed my parents in the process. My dad can't remember yesterday, and my mom had to take an early retirement to take care of him."

I stepped closer, aware that Jessica watched me closely. She was probably ready to step in if I attempted murder. When I stepped toward April's face, I said, "So if you know anything that we need to know, I suggest you tell us. The cops are on their way." It was a lie, but I had a cell phone and could make it a reality. And I planned to, the moment I got my hands on my son. No way was I leaving the house without Jacob.

April's face crumpled. She began to wring her hands, tears streaming down her blotched face. "She—she told me I'd better disappear, that you were going to take Justin from me. She gave me some money."

"Who?" I stepped closer, nearly touching noses with her. Behind me, I heard Jessica stir, poised and ready to stop me from violence. Funny, in the past, it had always been the other way around. "Who told you that? Who gave you money?"

"I—I don't know her name!"

"Where did you get Jacob?" I shouted in her face.

She cringed back from the fury in my eyes. "My—our lawyer handled the details. It was an independent adoption, a young girl who didn't want to keep her baby. She didn't want to be involved, or for us to know who she was."

"I feel sorry for your lawyer," I snarled. "Because I have a feeling he's going to be out of a job when they investigate him."

"I didn't know," she whispered, tears flowing down her face. "I swear. I didn't know that someone had taken him."

"Well, now you do, don't you? And I want to know the name of the woman who told you."

"I don't know, I really don't!"

Jessica caught my hand before it connected with the sobbing woman's face. "Describe her," Jessica ordered, slowly lowering my arm to my side. She wisely held her grip.

"She—she had blond hair and blue eyes," April said haltingly. She glanced at Jessica, and her eyes got wider. "Like your sister. She looked like your sister."

Shock thrummed through me. I could feel the same shock echoing through Jessica. Hoarsely, I asked, "Like Justin? Did she look like our son?"

The shock became a group reaction. April swayed on her feet, then steadied herself. "Yes, yes. Now that you mentioned it, she did look like Justin. . . ."

A murderous mixture of anger and sorrow welled inside me. I didn't know why, but I knew whom. My mother was somehow involved in this horrendous mess.

"Jessica, go get Jacob. We're leaving."

But Jessica wasn't as far gone as I was. She remained calm enough to point out the obvious.

"Hilary, he doesn't know you. We can't just grab him and take him kicking and screaming with us. You don't want to traumatize him, do you?"

"Then we'll take April with us," I announced. "Get your purse," I told April. "We're going to the police right now, and you're going to tell them everything you know."

At the police station, Jessica had to physically restrain me when they brought my mother in for questioning. If I hadn't convinced them to call the district attorney to confirm my story, I don't think they would have believed me. But together, with April's halting testimony and Dex McFarlane's confirmation of the pending investigation, they issued a warrant and brought in my mother.

Her tearful story made me go cold with a murderous rage. I'd never wanted to kill anyone before, but by the time she finished, I believe that I could have killed her.

The more she talked, the more everything began to make a twisted kind of sense. At several points, I couldn't resist interrupting her and forcing her to tell the truth, however horrible it was.

"He—he didn't want anyone to find out about our affair," Mom told everyone in a shaky, defensive voice. "Kit—Dr. Bernard told me he would never leave his wife."

"Even when you told him you were pregnant with me?" I asked through gritted teeth.

"Yes, even then. He said he'd deny everything if I came out with it." Mom's chin came up a hair. "I wasn't about to let anyone know how foolish I had been to believe that he loved me."

"Dad never knew," Jessica stated shrewdly. "Did he, Mom?"

Mom shook her head. "After a while, I realized that I'd made a mistake, that I didn't love him, so I buried the entire thing."

"Until I got pregnant," I cut in, tasting bitter hatred. "Then you were afraid I'd have a boy, and that he would be born with hemophilia, and that someone might guess the truth."

She looked straight at me, as if willing me to believe this one small thing. "I was afraid for you, Hilary. I knew what Kit was capable of. I was afraid of what he might do to protect his marriage and his career. He told me to discourage you from having children."

"Didn't work," I said, clasping my hands to keep them from her cold-hearted throat. "So I had Jacob, and Dr. Bernard figured out a way to make him disappear so his secret remained a secret. But you knew, didn't you, Mother? You were gone when the house blew up, so you knew it was going to happen."

I remembered what Dad had said about her insisting he stay in the living room. "You meant for Dad to die, too, didn't you? You had already taken Jacob out of the house, convinced Dad that he was sleeping, and you wanted that blast to kill Dad." Behind me, I heard Jessica moan in shock.

Mom looked down at her hands folded in her lap, probably to hide her shame. "Yes," she whispered. "I wanted him to die. When—when Kit and I had our affair, I realized I wasn't in love with Wesley."

"Wouldn't a divorce have been simpler?" Jessica asked in a biting voice. "You're a sick woman. I'm ashamed that you're my mother, and I pray to God that I didn't get any of your sick genes."

The investigating cops stared down at their shoes; uncomfortable with the pain I'm sure they could literally feel emanating from us.

I took a great, gulping gasp, feeling the pain arrow straight into my heart. My mother . . . oh, God, it was too awful. But I knew that it was true.

"You helped blow up my house and let me believe my baby had died to cover up your twisted affair with Dr. Bernard? Is that how it went, Mother? You're blaming it on him, but you were there. You helped him. You knew. And you're my mother."

"He's your father, Hilary," she said, as if she were afraid he wouldn't get his share of the blame.

50

"Wesley is my father," I shot back. "He raised me, believed that I was his daughter. Now, because of you, he's a shell of the man he used to be. How could you live with yourself?" How could Dr. Bernard live with himself? How could I have worked for a man capable of such a heinous crime? Obviously, he cared nothing for me, or his own grandson." I felt sick inside, just knowing I was the spawn of such evil.

Despite Dr. Bernard's vehement denial that he had anything to do with the kidnapping, attempted murder, and arson of my home, the jury believed my mother's testimony. The fact that she cut a deal with them in lieu of her testimony against her former lover, still leaves a bitter taste in my mouth. The five-year sentence wasn't justice in my mind—just a joke.

Dad moved in with us, and I hired a nurse to stay with him during the day. Jacob visits us on weekends and holidays, but we're taking it very slowly. Now that I realize April reacted as any threatened mother might react at the thought of losing her child, we manage to maintain a harmonious relationship for Jacob's sake. I know that she loves Jacob as I love him, and together, we are keeping his well-being in mind. When we think the time is right, we will tell him that I'm his biological mother and let him decide where he wants to live. If he chooses Stephen and me, I can live with that, and April claims she can, too.

I got tested and found out I was a carrier of the disease that Jacob suffers, and was counseled against having any more children. When the realization gets me down, I remember how lucky I am to have Candace and Jacob.

Someday, I will have the sad task of explaining to them how they will likely pass the disease on to their offspring, but that's years away. In the meantime, I'm going to enjoy the second chance God has given me.

THE END